Stretch, Swallow & Stare

VERONIKA MARTENOVA CHARLES

Stoddart
Kids
TORONTO • NEW YORK

*We acknowledge the Canada Council for the Arts and the
Ontario Arts Council for their support of our publishing program.*

Published in Canada in 1999 by
Stoddart Kids,
a division of Stoddart Publishing Co. Limited
34 Lesmill Road
Toronto, ON M3B 2T6
Tel (416) 445-3333 Fax (416) 445-5967
E-mail Customer.Service@ccmailgw.genpub.com

Published in the United States in 1999 by
Stoddart Kids,
a division of Stoddart Publishing Co. Limited
180 Varick Street, 9th Floor
New York, New York 14207
Toll free 1-800-805-1083
E-mail gdsinc@genpub.com

Distributed in Canada by
General Distribution Services
325 Humber College Blvd.,
Toronto, ON M9W 7C3
Tel (416) 213-1919 Fax (416) 213-1917
E-mail Customer.Service@ccmailgw.genpub.com

Distributed in the United States by
General Distribution Services
85 River Rock Drive, Suite 202
Buffalo, New York 14207
Toll free 1-800-805-1083
E-mail gdsinc@genpub.com

Canadian Cataloguing in Publication Data

Charles, Veronika Martenova
Stretch, Swallow & Stare

ISBN 0-7737-3098-2

I. Title.

PS8555.H42242S77 1998   jC813'.54   C98-930516-3
PZ7.C42St 1998

Printed and bound in Hong Kong, China

Stretch was not like other people. She was very tall. Not only that, she could stretch her body taller than the tallest tree. Stretch was kind too, but people only saw that she was different.

Now, one night, some children vanished from their homes. No explanation, no clues, they simply disappeared. People were frightened. And who did they blame? One look at Stretch and they decided she had something to do with it. They greeted her with silence. They whispered behind her back. Finally, unhappy and hurt, Stretch ran away deep into the forest.

It was peaceful there and the air was warm and sweet. Suddenly she heard a voice. "Excuse me!" it said.

Stretch looked around and saw a small boy who didn't seem one bit afraid of her.

"I'm Ira," said the boy, "and I'm looking for my older sister, Kate. Last night she disappeared and I've got to find her. She is the only family I have. Tell me, did you see her?"

"I didn't," replied Stretch. Her heart went out to the boy. "Poor child," she thought. "So small! And now there's no one bigger to look after him." Then she told Ira about the other children who had vanished the same way his sister did.

"Can you help me find Kate?" Ira asked.

"I'll try," she said, making herself shorter. "If we find your sister, maybe we'll find the other children too!"

Together, they left the woods.

Before long, they came to a village. It was carnival day. There were games and rides and crowds of people. In the square an eating contest had begun, and on the stage a short but very large woman was eating everything in sight.

"I wonder who she is," Stretch whispered to Ira.

"They call her Swallow," said a girl beside them. "Keep watching and you'll see why."

As Swallow downed plates of pasta, potatoes, and pies, sandwiches, sausages, and cookies, her body expanded like a balloon. The crowd whistled and clapped, but only until she was declared the winner. Then the audience made fun of her and called her names.

Stretch and Ira turned away.

When they left the village, they found
Swallow sitting by the road. She was crying.
They tried to cheer her, but it was no use.

Finally, Ira had to ask. "Did you see
my older sister? She disappeared last night
and I've got to find her. She's the only family
I have."

"I didn't," replied Swallow. She wiped
her eyes. "Poor child," she thought. "So
skinny! And now there's no one to feed him."

"Other children are missing too," Stretch
told her. "Would you like to come with us
and help find them?"

"Oh, yes," said Swallow. "I'd love to
help. Nobody here would miss me anyway."

Together, they continued down the road.

By and by they came to some mountains. Among the boulders they saw a woman sitting on the ground. As they came closer, she hid her face from them.

"Why do you turn away?" asked Ira.

"I must! My eyes are so strong they burn through anything I look at," replied the woman. "That's why I am called Stare. I live here because people are afraid of me."

"Use my sock to cover your eyes," Ira offered. "Then you won't hurt us." Stretch and Swallow each added something and soon a thick blindfold was in place.

"I'm looking for my older sister," Ira told Stare. "She disappeared and I've got to find her. Kate is the only family I have. Could you see where she is?"

"Only this morning I saw a fortress far from here. Inside there were many children. Kate might be one of them. Then she thought, "Poor child. Such weak eyes! And now there's no one to show him the way."

"Would you like to come and be our guide?" Stretch asked.

"I'd be glad to," said Stare. "At last I'll have someone to talk to." Together, they walked on.

Stare led the group to the base of a mountain. "There's an underground passage to the fortress and it begins here." She took off her blindfold and focused on the ground in front of her. Rocks began to crumble and explode. Bang! Whoosh! When the dust settled, they spied the entrance to a tunnel. "Follow me," said Stare, and led the way down.

Underground it was dark and damp. In places the path was washed away by a river, so Stretch helped them over it. When falling stones blocked the passage, Stare cleared them out of the way. And when they were tired and cold, Swallow wrapped her arms around her friends to warm them. At last they saw daylight and emerged on the other side of the mountains.

In front of them, its black shape piercing the sky, stood the fortress.

"So tall!" thought Stretch. "Even I can't reach that high."

Stare peered through her blindfold and thought, "I've never seen walls this thick! Even I can't burn through them."

The sun was sliding behind the horizon as the four friends crossed the drawbridge and stopped in front of a huge iron gate. It was locked. "Now what do we do?" wondered Ira.

As if to answer, the gate creaked open.

The four friends entered cautiously. But as soon as they were inside, the gate behind them slammed shut with a loud clang. There was nowhere to go but up the winding stairs that waited before them.

They passed through dark corridors and chambers, and everywhere, sprawled on floors and slumped against walls, were sleeping children. Ira searched among them for Kate.

"There she is!" he cried, his heart pounding. He tried to wake her, but she remained in a deep sleep.

Softly at first, growing louder and louder, the walls began to echo with the sound of heavy footsteps. Then the dark figure of a wizard appeared.

"Why have you come?" he demanded.

"I . . . I . . . came for my sister," said Ira, trying to remain calm. "What have you done to these children? Why are they asleep?"

"I live on their dreams, you nosy little urchin. That's why I stole them and put them under my spell," growled the wizard. "Your sister has the sweetest dreams of all. You will not take her anywhere."

"But she is all I . . ."

"How dare you think you and these useless misfits can walk in here and take her back!" cried the wizard, growing angrier by the second. "Even if you watched over her every minute of every day, I could snatch her away any time I chose. Why, you can't even look after two socks at once!"

"He didn't lose his other sock. He gave it to me out of kindness," said Stare, growing angry too.

"And don't be so sure we're useless," added Stretch. "Protecting Ira's sister from your powers shouldn't be so hard."

"Test us tonight and see," taunted Swallow. "We will guard her while you try to get her back. If we still have her by morning, will you let us all go free?"

"A contest! How amusing," the wizard laughed cruelly. "Very well, I'll play your little game. But I warn you. By the time the sun's first rays touch this floor, the girl will be in my possession. I will win, and you will pay with your lives!" He led them to a chamber, and then he was gone.

Ira slumped down beside his sister, suddenly drowsy and weak. He strained to keep his eyes open and dug his fingernails into his arms to stay awake. Stretch wearily wound herself around them, while Swallow wedged her body into the doorway. Stare kept watch at the window.

"Let's sing to stay awake," pleaded Ira. And they did. But even as they sang, the wizard's power pulled them closer to sleep.

It was past midnight when Stretch awoke to a cold gust of air on her face. She shuddered and looked around. Moonlight shone on the empty floor beside her. Kate was gone!

"Wake up! Wake up!" she urged her sleeping friends. Swallow and Stare started, but Ira slumbered on and nothing would wake him.

Stare ran to the window and looked out. "I see her!" she said. "She is very far away. Many miles from here is a lagoon. In that lagoon is a giant shell. In that shell is Ira's sister. We must get her back before sunrise!"

Though hesitant to leave Ira, Stretch lowered her body down from the window so that Swallow and Stare could run along it. Then she picked them up and strode toward the lagoon, each step covering a mile.

When they reached the shore, Stare looked into the water. "It's too deep," she said. "Far deeper than Stretch can reach. What are we going to do?"

"Maybe I can help," said Swallow. She lay on the ground and put her mouth to the water. She drank and drank, her body swelling in all directions.

Swallow drank until the lagoon was dry.

The giant shell rested in a sandy hollow and shimmered in the moonlight. Stretch climbed down to it and tried to pull it apart. She tugged and pulled until her fingers were raw. When the shell finally split open, Stretch gently lifted Kate out and carried her up to the shore.

As the sky turned pale, Stare gazed into the distance and gasped. "The wizard is on his way up to the chamber!" she cried. "We'll never make it back in time!"

"Maybe I can!" said Stretch. "With only the girl to carry I can run faster than the wind. Stay with Swallow until she can move again." Stretch took off like a bolt of lightning. "I'll come for you later," she promised as she sped away.

At the fortress the wizard broke into the room. "So!" he roared.
"Your friends got scared and left you!"

Ira opened his eyes and saw that he was alone. At the same time
he saw sunlight beginning to enter the chamber. Thinking fast, he
stuck out his foot so that the buckle on his shoe reflected the beams
back out the window.

"You haven't won yet!" he cried. "The sun's first rays still haven't touched the floor. My friends will be back. You'll see!"

At that moment, hands reached through the window and gently placed something at the wizard's feet. It was Ira's sister!

"It can't be!" the wizard screeched. He twisted in fury and sizzled with rage. Sparks flew as his anger began to destroy him. Flames rose, and from their center a raven appeared. It cawed wildly as it flew out the window and disappeared. The wizard's power had gone.

Kate began to stir. She opened her eyes and saw her brother. "Ira!" she cried, and rushed to embrace him.

Now, light poured freely in, chasing darkness from the place. The fortress came alive with sounds of children waking from their long sleep.

Stretch left to get Swallow and Stare and soon they were all back together.

"Will you come and live with us?" Ira asked them.

"We'll make sure you and all the children get safely to your homes," Stretch replied, "but we will not stay."

"The villagers wouldn't welcome us for long," added Swallow.

"Besides, we have each other now," said Stare.

"Yes!" they said together. "We have each other now."

Stretch, Swallow and Stare gathered the children around them and they began their journey home.

AUTHOR'S NOTE

The characters of Stretch, Swallow and Stare come from the most beloved Czech fairy tale, *The Long One, the Wide One and the Sharp-eyed One*. In the original version they are white male friends who, with their magical abilities, help a prince free his bride from an evil wizard. For me and generations of Czech children before the world became a global village, these characters were superheroes.

When I came to North America, I was surprised that there was no popular version of this tale, although there were some similarities in *The Wizard of Oz* and *The Five Chinese Brothers*. For many years I thought about retelling the story and about the three characters.

I tried to get beneath their skins in order to understand who they really were. It seemed to me that their alienation and social rejection was a result of their "wrong" body types. As I could perceive of them only from the present reality — our body-conscious, beauty-oriented culture — I decided they would ring more true if portrayed as women. This gave me an opportunity to create unique female individuals within the fairy tale genre. They became large, vulnerable heroines with much to offer.

I am happy I can pass on the magic of these characters as a gift from the cultural heritage of my birthplace to the children of my adopted land.